A BREACH OF SECURITY

A BREACH OF SECURITY

A Simon Serrailler Crime Story

Susan Hill

LONG BARN BOOKS

Copyright © Susan Hill 2014

PUBLISHED BY
LONG BARN BOOKS LTD

All Rights Reserved

Without limiting the rights under copyright reserved above, no part of this publication may be reproduced, stored in or introduced into a retrieval system, or transmitted in any form or by any means (electronic, mechanical, photocopying, recording or otherwise) without prior permission of both the copyright owner and the above publisher of this book.

Printed and bound in the UK by
JFDi Print Services Ltd.

ISBN: 978-1-902421-59-9

To
Simon Serrailler fans, everywhere.

1

'New bowler,' Sam said. Simon Serrailler had been lying on his back, panama hat tipped over his face. He had not exactly been asleep, just drifting, like the shreds of cloud across the deep blue sky. The previous bowler had been slow, effective at preventing more than the occasional dash of a single run, but dull to watch. Sam was padded up ready to go on, after four other men were out but it looked as if the day would be over before he got the chance. Now, however, the new bowler obviously meant business. He had handed his sweater to the umpire, paced about a bit, throwing the ball from hand to hand, and now he was bringing the field in close and tightening it.

'Only one man at the boundary?' Sam said. 'That's just arrogance.'

'I shouldn't be wishing our own bats out should I?'

'Of course you should, you want your turn at the crease, who doesn't?'

'Wish I was better then I'd move up the order a bit.'

'Nets, nets, nets.'

'I go to nets every week.'

'Listen, you are one of the best wicket-keepers I've ever seen in my life, outside of test cricket. You're not a bad batsman, you're solid, you know when to take a chance and let rip, and with serious practice you could move up maybe to five or six. But there's no one to touch you behind the wicket and you know it. Not a skill I've ever had.'

'Too tall.'

'Too tall.'

The slips leaned forwards as the bowler stalked down to his mark. People round the ground sat up and took notice. There was a random shout of 'Get on with it.'

This, Serrailler thought, was the perfect day off, a late June Sunday, warm but with the occasional slight breeze rippling the grass beyond the boundary, stirring the line of poplars. It was a fine ground, the crowd was good, the teams well matched. Sam might get to bat or he might not, but when his team came on to field, he would be in the spotlight. Serrailler did not flatter. He had seen few wicket-keepers to touch him, which was why he had made the junior county first eleven, in spite of his unfocused batting.

They were on their own, for the next week. Sam's mother, Cat Deerbon, had gone to a palliative care conference in Italy, where she was giving a paper, Hannah was away at her stage school, Felix was staying with a fellow chorister. In July, he would be away with the choir on a tour of Scandinavian Cathedrals. Arrangements did not always work out as well but asbestos had been found in

Simon's building in the Close, and he had had to leave his flat while it was stripped out. Cat had been delighted to give him a home in the farmhouse for as long as it took, and he was singing for his supper by looking after Sam while she was away. They got on well. Sam was easy-going, but Simon kept him on the right side of laziness. They liked each other's company, Sam was responsible if he had to be alone in the house, they ate together and shared the chores. Only Mephisto the cat showed his disapproval of his mistresses's absence by spending most of his time out hunting. Wookie, the Yorkshire terrier, had the kitchen sofa to himself and, in defiance of the house rule, sneaked upstairs and onto Sam's bed every night.

Exams were over, term ended the following week. Lafferton had been quiet, the police keeping pace, CID only tested by a spate of bicycle thefts and a hit and run case in which a popular local schoolteacher had been killed.

It was only a matter of time before the van driver was found.

Summer, Simon thought, blissful summer, and raised his hands above his head in appreciation of a six which hit a fast and accurate path straight through the stunned slip fielders, to an empty boundary. Sam groaned, seeing his own prospects of an innings recede further, and applause rippled round, as the batsman acknowledged his fifty up.

2

A couple of miles from the cricket ground, in the centre of Lafferton, more applause, and laughter, cheers and waves, as the Gay Pride march reached the town square. The sun had brought the crowds out, and the ice cream vans, the burger stands, the stray dogs, the children perched on shoulders. People ran alongside the floats, whose riders pelted them with paper flowers, sweets, confetti, bubbles. The bands at the front, in the middle, at the back and alongside played different music and the tunes clashed in the air between.

It was the third year of the Gay Pride Festival. The first had been received by Lafferton with a little uncertainty, a small amount of hostility, and a lot of amusement. Last year's parade had been called off after torrential rain and thunderstorms closed the streets. This year, everything was set fair. The marshals had organised things well, the minimal police presence was good humoured, with instructions for 'hands off' unless there was trouble, but there had been none, apart from the usual minor accidents and exaggerated reports of pickpockets working the crowds. One of the floats, half way through the procession, had managed to rig up a bath and shower with water spraying in a haphazard way onto a man lying dressed in a pink onesie and wearing a bubble wig. As it passed water shot sideways out of the connecting hose and drenched a couple of young men standing on the pavement. A few other people caught a light spray and jumped aside and a small boy shrieked with laughter. The man in the bath waved regally, at which one of the youths started to run alongside the float, shouting angry obscenities, his mate egging him on.

It was over in a few seconds, the boys merged back into the crowd and the procession carried on without a hiccup. No one referred to what had happened. No one looked round for the police. The general attitude seemed to be 'ignore them.' The sun shone.

In a cul de sac behind the square, Abbo Crowley and Dan Sturridge leaned against one another, helpless with laughter.

'Shut the fuck up. What the hell did you think you were playing about at?'

They had joined a group of a dozen others who had seen the incident through a gap between houses.

'Dweebs. The whole bloody point was not to go off at half-cock, not to get wound up, not to … ach, what's the use. Now listen, you, are you with us or not because if not, fuck off now, and if you are, will you listen and do as you're fuckin' told and not go off on one again? You know what the plan is, you know what your roles are, right?'

'Yes, boss, no boss, three bags full boss.' Abbo made a v sign.

'I'm ignoring that. OK, now listen up because we haven't got long ...'

They were not scruffy, they were smartly dressed, in dark blue open-necked shirts, dark blue chinos. Each one had a small badge in the shape of a bulldog pinned onto his lapel. Each one had shirt sleeves rolled up neatly. Each one had short, tidy hair. Each one wore heavy black boots, in a temperature more suited to sandals.

'We fan out until we reach the corner before the square, which is where the whole lot will start to slow down, waiting to get into place. It'll take quite a while. Half of us on the right, the others on the left. And then wait. Wait till my call. Wait and don't jump the gun like these two numpties. Wait and then, you're in. Remember, there aren't any cops and they've been scattered, but they're not idiots, the second they cotton on, they'll gang up and be onto us – we haven't got more than a few minutes. Don't get near any onlookers, avoid any kids or dogs like the plague, don't do anything except what you're meant to. Right?'

A mutter around the group. Smithy looked at his watch. They could hear the cacophony of bands, the shouting, the laughter, the cheers and whoops.

'Ponces. Effing gay scum.'

'Save it.'

'I don't known how they bloody dare. Pervs.'

'I said ...'

But the long hand of the watch touched the half hour.

'Go,' Smithy said. 'Move. Bulldogs ...'

'March!' The British Bulldogs shouted as one, turned, and set off to the end of the lane, where it joined the square, marching in time. Marching. Marching.

PC Beverley Holmes had a headache, brought on by too much sun. They were on duty for another four hours and she wouldn't get through it without a Nurofen. The parade had been noisy, everyone was good humoured, and she felt like lying down under the tree that shaded the slab of pathway where she was standing.

'Go off, why don't you?' Darren Jamieson said. 'You're no good to yourself like this. Get home, take a couple of meds and lie down with the curtains drawn. Mel's Mum gets these and they don't get better without you do something.'

'Thanks.'

'Well you're no good as you are.'

'So you said. OK, it's nearly done anyway... once they're all lined up in the square, it's just the judging and the presentations and then the party starts. We can spare you.'

'Yeah. Right, thanks then, Day... can you call in for me?'

'Consider it done.'

The floats had passed PC Beverley Holmes. She watched the end of the 'Gay Pride Hairdressers' on which two young women stood unsteadily trying to put the long hair of two young men in rollers and a bunch of pink balloons detached themselves from the back and sailed up into the sky, to a few scattered cheers. She had not wanted to be on duty. She was unhappy about the whole thing. What was there to be proud about? She paid lip service to the police diktats about tolerance and diversity and if people shut up about it, she didn't object to other lifestyles – they were wrong, her pastor was adamant, the teaching of the bible was crystal clear but probably none of these guys in the parade belonged to the church so let them get on with it. She kept her mouth shut at all times. She enjoyed her job, she wanted to rise a bit higher – just a bit, to sergeant, but not above. They would start a family in a couple of years and being a proper mother didn't sort with being a high ranking officer. Which was fine. Only if she said what she really thought, she could be out, crazy as it seemed, and she daren't risk it, however much she knew she ought to stand up for her faith.

'They're not doing anyone any harm,' Warren had said, a bit more relaxed about the whole thing than she was.

She didn't agree. There were families here this afternoon, families with children, enjoying the fun, but what sort of message were they getting from all this, what sort of hope did they have? Adults were adults, but she disagreed strongly with pushing the gay agenda down the throats of innocent kids.

'Hey, hey,' she said, watching the last float vanish out of sight. The road was a mess of pink streamers and paper darts and shaving foam that had been sprayed out of cans from the floats. So whose job was it to clear that lot up? The gay refuse disposal team?

Bev started to stroll up the road, looking out for Jim, who she was supposed to be paired with but who seemed to have disappeared.

The sun shone. 'On the just and the unjust,' she thought.

A second later, she heard a roar from the square.

Screams. Angry shouts. Bands grinding to a halt in mid-tune.

Bev ran. She turned into the main square as two other officers came pelting down from the opposite side. For a second or two, they stopped and tried to take in the scene. One man was lying on his back in the road below a float, two others, dressed in tutus, were kneeling beside him, in a pool of blood. On the float behind, three youths wearing navy shirts and trousers were punching and flailing at two men, who were struggling to get up and being beaten down again.

A float had tipped half onto its side while a number of men leaned and pushed, trying to prevent it from toppling completely over. People were trying to escape from the square, carrying children. An elderly couple were clinging to one another, not knowing which way to turn.

Sirens started to scream in the distance.

The man on the ground in the bubble wig had

blood pouring from his head. Bev knelt down beside him, next to a Community Support Officer, who was trying to staunch the flow. The man's face was already swelling with large contusions to his cheekbone and forehead.

'Apparently it was a short plank of wood with a nail in the end,' the CSO said. 'Not good.'

The man groaned and his eyes rolled up into his head. Bev felt his pulse, which was weak and thready. The blood was still flowing.

'Who was it?'

'Youths apparently, posse of them, but nobody seems to know anything much. Ambulance needs to step on it.'

From the float ahead came sudden screams of pain and fear.

'Where the hell is everyone?' Bev said. 'Listen, you hold on here, try and stop the blood flow, I'm getting up there.'

'Watch yourself, maybe wait till ....'

'Till what?' Bev shouted, already starting to clamber onto the float. Three of the blue-shirted youths were hammering into two men in fancy dress. 'Bull-dogs, Bull-dogs,' came with each punch. Another cheered them on, shouting abuse. People on the ground were standing in shock, somehow paralysed with uncertainty.

Bev jumped on one of the youths, arm round his throat, and dragged him off the victims, only to receive a punch in the stomach which had her staggering back, winded. She recovered quickly, and pulled the youth round. His face was ugly with excitement, triumph, and loathing.

'Get the fuck off me, cop, you get your hands off ...'

But Beverley was five feet eleven and solid, with a black belt in karate, and assault training. The boy, with his British Bulldog badge unpinned on his lapel, stood no chance. His mates had jumped off the float and were running.

'Grab them, hold onto them,' Bev yelled. At first, no one did anything, so that they got a head start as they ducked and dived away through the rapidly thinning crowd, but then, two of the 'Hairdressers for Gay Pride' gave chase. Bev had her youth in an arm lock. He had twice spat in her face, and mouthed a lot of filthy abuse, which she could easily ignore. But she wondered if she could keep hold, make an arrest, drag the youth off the float and pin him down, without any help. Where were the rest of the team? Where was back-up, for heaven's sake?

Navy-shirt kicked out at her and caught the side of her leg with his boot. The blow was searingly painful and it was as much as Bev could do not to let him go.

It seemed like hours before another PC jumped onto the float and took over. Meanwhile, the paramedics had reached the man with the head injury and at last, re-inforcements came screaming into the square.

3

A spin bowler had disposed of four batsmen in quick succession, giving Sam his chance.

In the car on the way home, he banged his hand again on the door frame.

'Come on, you didn't score but you weren't out either … you got to walk off when the stumps were pulled – no shame.'

'I should have gone for that last but one, I should have had a swing at it.'

'Nope, that ball would have hit the middle, smack, and the bails would have flown … knowing when to leave a ball alone is as important …'

'I know, I know.'

'So stop re-running your innings. You did fine.'

Sam threw himself back in his seat. 'Stop laughing.'

'I feel like laughing. I feel very perky, actually. A couple of cold beers, steaks to cook, maybe another beer and there might even be a good film.'

'Just not crime.'

'Just not.'

'Hey, did you hear all those sirens?'

'Yup. Not my problem.'

'Accident I suppose.'

'Usually. Only I'm not letting work cross my mind till Monday morning.'

He was finishing his first icy lager when Sam shouted from the Den. 'You might want to see this.'

Serrailler wandered from the kitchen. The television was turned to the regional news.

'Who are these 'British Bulldogs'?'

'Haven't heard of them,' Simon said. A video of the march and its bloody aftermath was rolling out across the screen. And then came the complaints. He watched, groaning, as one after another, people spoke about lack of police presence, the length of time taken for those who were there to get to the scene, and so on.

'Is that true?'

'I'm afraid it probably is. Trouble is, we don't want a big show of police strength at these things, it gives out the wrong signal and it isn't usually needed ... we haven't had trouble before, and we always have back-up on call ... no one could have expected these yobbos to kick off.'

'Looks planned.'

'Oh yes, they'll have gone there spoiling for a fight.'

'The injured man, Gavin Day, is in a serious condition, with major head injuries. Doctors at Bevham General Hospital say it is too soon to predict whether he has suffered brain damage. Seven other people were hurt in the incident, two of them seriously. They are detained in hospital, the others were allowed home after treatment on the scene.'

'Will you have to go in?'

'Unlikely. Mike Philipot is in charge this weekend and he'll have spoken to the Acting Chief. But there'll be a big inquest on Monday morning. Can you come and do a salad dressing and lay the kitchen table, Sam?'

Sam had started to take an interest in cooking. Simon had shown him how to make a good omelette one evening and it had gone from there, but Sam had made him swear not to mention it to Cat. 'What, because she might make you get the supper every evening?'

'No. Just ... you know.'

Simon did. Sam was embarrassed. Sixteen years old and testosterone had a lot to answer for.

'Can we watch episode three of *Homeland?* Doesn't count as cops.'

'Fine.'

But though he was gripped by the series, Serrailler's mind swerved back every so often to the pictures on the news, the violence, the injured who had been enjoying their parade, the hatred and venom on the faces of the two youths, caught briefly on the scene video-d by a bystander with a good smart-phone, the viciousness of the attack. He doubted if they would get good enough ID from the blurred pictures but it was a start. British Bull-dogs. Lafferton was an unlikely centre for any Far Right trouble-makers. They would almost certainly have come either from Bevham, or further afield.

He got another beer. He would watch the late-night news after Sam had gone to bed, for any update and to check out the video again. He felt sickened. On Monday morning, after a full briefing, he would probably feel worse.

4

The initial debriefing on the events at the Parade had been to a full Conference room of uniform and CID who had been on duty, as well as those who were at work, all attending. The Acting Chief Constable was in London at an ACPO conference on security but had spoken to the Superintendent in overall charge. It had not, by his account, been a comfortable call.

'Heads will roll,' a DC muttered.

'You're kidding. When do they ever?'

'Well someone fucked up.'

'Not really. Who could have predicted that little lot? We were supposed to be a low-key, friendly presence on the streets not an armed response unit.'

Before they dispersed, the Super had raised a hand for quiet.

'One more thing. I'd like to single out a PC for special mention this morning. Beverley Holmes showed resourcefulness, quick thinking, cool-headedness and courage. She had no idea whether any of her colleagues were behind to back her up, she had no idea who was causing the trouble on the float, whether they had any form of weapon or if they were likely to turn on her. Nevertheless, she put herself in danger, without a second's thought. She gave emergency help to the injured and arrested and detained a potentially violent offender. The Acting Chief has asked me to pass on congratulations Bev, and I know everyone in this room feels the same.'

Beverley was pulled to her feet, and the room erupted in applause.

'Deserves a medal.'

'Bet she gets one,' a DC said.

News came in later in the day that the

condition of the injured man was grave, but stabilising. It was still not clear whether or not he had suffered brain damage.

The station was in shock, the general mood low. Lafferton police were being blamed for everything by the media, and the public the tabloids were successfully rousing to even greater anger, and whoever had decided to have a small presence on the streets for the Gay Pride Parade was being called to own up and resign.

Serrailler tried to sort through the minor items for his attention, and set two CID on the hunt for the British Bulldogs – where they came from, who was in charge, what their agenda was, plus any identification from the video. People who had remained in the square were asked if they had taken any pictures and if so, to e-mail them in.

Just after five o'clock, he took a call from the Acting Chief.

'Keep next Thursday blocked out, Simon.

Major Gardiner and two of his officers are coming over. He contacted me earlier.'

'Ah.'

'Indeed. I want you, Mike Philpott, and possibly one other. Apart from whoever will take notes, that has to be all. Strictly on a need-to-know thereafter, understood?'

'Yes.'

'We can't risk anything going wrong this time.'

The Prince of Wales Own West Country Fusiliers had recently returned from one of the last tours of Afghanistan, and the regiment was due to parade its Colours through Lafferton, ending at the Cathedral for a service. The march had last taken place three years previously, when there had been large crowds and no trouble but as of yesterday afternoon, the simple and straightforward advance plan for securing it had been torn up.

The meeting began on the stroke of nine.

The Major brought one officer, Captain Spicer. The Acting Chief came in at the start, to make the introductions, before leaving to take charge of a disciplinary hearing in another force.

'DCS Simon Serrailler, I think you know. Superintendent Mike Philpott. Inspector Ian Finch from Armed Response.'

'And Alison Barber, my secretary, taking the notes.' Simon added, after the Chief had left. Why were some of the high-ups always keen to make support staff invisible?

'Right. None of us expected to be here this morning but you are all fully aware of the appalling and rather surprising incidents at Lafferton's Gay Pride March. Frankly, we've never had anything like this happen and we have a number of annual parades and so forth, ranging from cubs and scouts to the Remembrance Day Parade. We've even had a Welcome Parade for Lafferton Rovers when they won the football cup. Nothing has ever gone wrong. These events are always good humoured, well organised and pass off without incident. St John's ambulance always attend. We have low-key police presence and yesterday should have been no different. I wasn't on duty so I didn't see what happened at first hand, but I've caught up fully, I've studied the video footage. One thing to say is that if I had been in charge, the number of police on duty would almost certainly have been the same. But they could have been better organised, spaced out along the route and with more in the square itself. When the trouble broke out, officers had to race from the end of the High Street and even further away, they were out of touch with one another and there was a certain amount of confusion.'

'I'd put it a bit more strongly, and I have also looked at the footage,' the Major said. 'It was chaos.'

'Well, whatever words are used, I'm sure we all agree that the reaction on the ground was poor and the whole thing a lamentable example of disorganisation.'

'And you had no warning at all? And you have no idea who or what this group of individuals stand for or where they sprang from?'

Serrailler resented being addressed and cross-questioned as if he were a very junior officer being disciplined but he took a breath and shook his head.

'No warning of any kind. Colleagues in CID are now investigating the group – British Bulldogs, as they call themselves, and I expect them to report back very soon. They shouldn't be hard to trace – they're probably fairly local. I'll share the info with you the moment I have any.'

Major Gardiner nodded. 'Let's put yesterday aside for the time being. I'd like to go through our order and timings as they stand – you may comment as I go along if you think we need to change anything.'

'Please go ahead.'

'I have everything on my laptop. I'm going to put up the route plan on the screen there, and the schedule in a sidebar.'

'Do you need anything else, Major?' Alison asked quietly.

'Thanks, I'm organised.'

Simon gave her a smile. He needed Alison, probably the best secretary he had ever had. She had picked up on the complexities of his work and diary, as well as on his preferences in almost everything, within a few weeks of arriving eighteen months before, and now he thought she probably knew what he would do, say, think, before he did. She had taken a lot of the admin off his hands as a matter of course, she had never had a day off other than for scheduled holidays, and never come into work with anything other than a smile and a willing attitude. If he was in the middle of a complex operation, she would stay late without being asked, and when he was away, she covered everything.

A large scale map of Lafferton appeared on the screen. Major Gardiner clicked the arrow onto the Territorial Army barracks, which had a large parade ground at the back.

'Our vehicles will be parked off here. We assemble in the TA drill ground at 9.45. March off at 9.55. Here is the route, the same as in previous years.'

The arrow moved out onto the side road which led from the barracks, followed along to the junction, turned left, and headed down the main road leading to the centre.

'Street has open access to the public on both sides, and we anticipate crowds, particularly this year after our tour and the loss of five men in Afghanistan. We turn into the square here... the dais is placed here ... covered if the weather is inclement.'

'Do we have royalty?'

The Major hesitated.

'You're in a police station and our meeting is confidential,' Serrailler said.

'We have royalty. The usual arrangements –liaison between us, you, and the royal office.'

Simon sighed.

'I fully understand that when we have royalty special security arrangements are always in force but as you yourself know, those arrangements, erm, vary, according to the rank of the visitor. If it were the Queen ...'

'It is not Her Majesty the Queen, this is, you know, a Prince of Wales own regiment.'

'So if Prince Charles ...'

'His Royal Highness the Prince of Wales will be our guest on the day. I must insist that the information remains inside this room ...'

How old are you, Simon thought? The Major was probably forty and looked younger. How can a man of your age, even given your position, be so bloody pompous?

'That,' he said, 'is perfectly understood.'

The Superintendent was looking hard at a mark on the table. They could say what they thought to one another later.

'After the Salute and march past, we will stand to attention in the square here... His Royal Highness leaves by car for the Cathedral ... at ten twenty two, we turn sharp right and continue up via Wren Street and Cathedral Lane, to the Cathedral. We will enter by the East door, and the Service of thanksgiving commences. His Royal Highness leaves, we leave and march back to the TA base where we have refreshments before heading away.'

He looked up.

'Quite straightforward, but with a lot of attention to detail required to cover every possible eventuality. I take it you will bring in officers from outside, Chief Superintendent? You won't have enough of your own. It will be necessary to have armed response on stand-by close to the barracks and again at the Cathedral.'

'If you'll forgive me, Major, that is a matter for the police but I assure you, your security on the day, as well as that of the public, is our top priority. Mike?'

The Superintendent stood up and went over to the screen. 'I'll use my finger to point, if you don't mind. We will have police at all key places on the route of the march ... as Simon says, we have to protect the public – crowds on the streets, people leaning out of windows and so forth. We have to secure the streets around the square, we need to have our strongest presence in the square itself, and then again, outside the Cathedral. There will also be CID inside it during the service. In addition of course, royal protection officers will be looking after the Prince. You're right that we may have to call on the adjacent force for extra men, but we can't have an equal number of police officers everywhere. Presumably, the TA barracks and parade ground will not be open to any members of the public, other than those civilians who work there and will have their own clearance?'

The Major nodded.

'So we will concentrate on the route and the square. You are your own security within the barracks premises ...'

'We need some police as well.'

'Can you explain why?'

'Because we will be concentrating on the job in hand.'

'Fine, but if by a remote chance there were to be a problem within the perimeter of the TA area, you would naturally deal with it. It is remote. The general public won't know where you assemble and set off.'

'Mike ... sorry but that is pretty obvious to anyone who knows Lafferton, and anyone who has been to a previous Parade. It won't be secret information, even if we don't actually put it in the papers.'

'Point taken. But I still feel that, given the usual need to make maximum use of limited resources, police presence can be – well, let's say 'minimal' at the barracks.'

The meeting lasted an hour and before the end, stiff politeness had turned icy.

'I don't know what the man expects,' Mike Philpott said, walking back upstairs with Serrailler. 'He knows as much as we do about cutbacks.'

'He was just pulling rank. Don't worry, we'll

deploy officers as well as we possibly can, he won't be unhappy on the day.'

'Heard any more about these Bulldogs?'

'No, but I think,' Simon said, as someone put his head out of the CID room door and beckoned, 'that I'm about to.'

The youth who had been arrested by Bev Holmes had been released on bail. His name was Duncan Leary. He had refused to answer questions other than to give name and age, and when asked about his part in the violence, the names of the others or the nature of the organisation 'British Bulldogs' he had simply remained silent or shaken his head.

But the CID research had come up with bits and pieces.

'So far as we can discover, there's nothing 'British' about them, in the sense that they're any sort of national organisation,' DC Callum McCalister said. 'They don't seem to have spread much outside the county, and they have been spreading propaganda leaflets around

Bevham, and in a couple of other places. They hand them out on the street and in shops, outside schools and so forth and scarper if anyone starts to ask questions.'

'What's their agenda, as if we didn't know...?'

'They're racist but it's all in the sub-text – chiefly, they're anti all forms of immigration by what they call 'non-ethnic British.' They're homophobic, don't approve of any form of gay rights, though they say they're fine about it all so long as it's 'a private matter.''

'Ha.'

'They are 'proudly supportive of Jewish culture and think anti-Semitisim should be cracked down on hard.''

'Surprising.'

'Unless it's a case of 'read my lips.''

'What are they *for*?'

'British traditions, British homeland, British culture, Britain for the British, marriage, family, women in the home. Respect for British history. I'm trying to get hold of an actual leaflet but apparently, they're pretty amateur – done by a corner printing bureau on cheapo green paper, and spelling and punctuation classes happened when they weren't in school.'

'Any names?'

'No, only the guy who was arrested. Average age seems to be around 20, male, white, smartly presented ... they're anxious not to look like yobbos.'

'Even if they behave like them. OK, thanks. Keep at it. Maybe get over to Bevham, go round the print shops, newsagents, ask about. Did we get anything on camera ... there must have been a heck of a lot of people taking pictures on smartphones, someone must have got a recognisable image. Get the press office to do an appeal ... Radio Bevham and the Gazette, even try local TV, see if they'll put it out. Any news of the guy they beat up?'

'Stable.'

'Which means sweet F.A. OK, thanks guys. Let's get out there.'

5

He waited in the car while Sam went into the *Taste of India* to collect their take-away. It was gone eight – Simon had been kept back at work by reports of a baby's body having been found under a seat on The Hill. Sam had been at nets.

'So,' he said, climbing back in, 'all here.' He patted the brown paper carrier. 'And I got some chips as well.'

'For heaven's sake, Sambo, we ordered enough for four already – you don't need chips.'

'I always need chips.'

Sam was only an inch off Simon in height already and Cat complained that he outgrew his trousers and shoes every six weeks. He ate hugely, would sleep the clock round if he could. Simon remembered the stage, when he had seemed not to fit into his own skin. It had felt like being a character in a fairy story.

'Listen, something I remembered. You know these British Bulldog guys?'

'Go on.'

'And you know Adam Warren?'

'Seam bowler?'

'Yup, and you know his brother Greg?'

'Sam, get on with it!'

'Sorry... well Greg is one.'

'What, a Bulldog?'

'Apparently...'

'How do you know this?'

'Adam was talking about. He says they're scum, only Greg's such a dork he doesn't realise.'

'OK, I need to talk to him.'

'Well don't quote me, I don't know anything.'

'Oh yes, great attitude Sam.'

'Yeah, but you know.'

'Yeah but, you told me. Do you expect me to do nothing?'

'No.'

'We don't reveal our sources, it's fine.'

'You wouldn't need to, they'll put two and two together.'

'Thought you said he was a dork.'

Later, mopping up the last of the Chicken Korma and basmati with their naan bread, Simon went through the scenario in his mind before mentioning it again. He got a beer out of the fridge and offered one to Sam.

'No thanks. I keep trying to get the taste of beer but I can't.'

'Probably a good thing.'

'Glass of red wine mind you ...'

'One. Small glass.'

Sam poured the last of the Merlot Simon had opened the previous night. '*Homeland*?'

'Before that ...listen Sam, it's pretty serious to name someone you know? These guys assaulted an innocent man very violently – make that, several innocent men, actually, only the others were luckier. Not to mention abuse and provocation and the rest ... we need their names, and maybe this Greg Warren could give them to us but before I make the call and he's brought in, just think hard. You have to be sure. What exactly did Adam say?'

'We were talking about the gay parade and he said, 'Greg's one of the Bulldogs, only he wasn't there on Saturday, he was at Sarah's wedding with the rest of us and a bloody good job.'

'Anything else?'

'Said he didn't know what Greg was messing about at – I mean, their Dad's a Vicar, their Mum teaches scripture at the Eric Anderson Comp, they wouldn't think like that, Adam doesn't think like that. Only I said, Greg's a bit weird. Always was. But you don't have to arrest him, you haven't got anything on him, he was at their cousin's wedding, right?'

'Questioning isn't arresting. I'll make sure it's clear he isn't under suspicion regarding Saturday's stuff but unless CID have any stronger leads he will be questioned, Sam. Has to be.'

'So he'd be a criminal if he said he was a member?'

'No. It isn't a proscribed organisation under the Terrorism Act.'

'How do you know?'

'Because I am very familiar with the list. Chances are this is a pretty local, small scale group – nasty little vermin, marching under the general banner of fascism. But whatever, they'll have the book thrown at them and we need names and addresses. So ... '

Serrailler looked across the table at his nephew. Sam looked back. Then he pulled a newspaper across, got out his pen and wrote in a margin.

'The police don't have friends, do they?' he said, shoving it over to Simon.

'Adam Warren, Holy Cross Vicarage, Blenheim Road. Addy.warren4000@gmail.com'

CID had drawn a blank with any further information. There was no trace of the British Bulldogs on the internet, extensive questioning in Lafferton, Bevham, and among adjacent police forces had yielded a blank, and the youths who had been involved in the violence had melted into the ether.

The usual course regarding Sam's information would have been for Simon to send whoever was free in CID out to Holy Cross Vicarage, but as his route to and from the police station went close to Blenheim Road, and to pacify Sam, Serrailler stopped off there himself, early the following evening. The Vicar was in. Gregory was almost eighteen and parental authority was not needed in order for Simon to question him, but out of courtesy, he explained briefly what the visit was about to his father. Philip Warren sighed.

'Frankly, Superintendent, nothing would surprise me. Gregory is not a bad boy I'm fairly sure, but he is a weak one and he's too easily led. He is impressed by anyone who throws his weight about, or has too much money, or gives an air of knowing a lot. I have never heard of these people but certainly you should talk to my son. I was horrified by what happened on Saturday. I can guarantee that Greg was not actually there but not anything more. He's watching television I daresay – and that's another thing. I'll fetch him. But may I just ask what – or who – led you to him in relation to all this?'

'I'm afraid I can't answer that, Vicar. I'm sorry but ...'

'No, no, of course you can't. Forget I asked. Makes no odds anyway.'

Greg Warren came in looking terrified, biting the skin round his nails, his gaze flicking to Serrailler and off again.

'Sit down, please.'

He hesitated, then did so, on the edge of the chair. He bent forwards. Sat back.

From the moment he had walked in, Simon knew that he had only to become serious, polite but unfriendly, and ask a few unpleasantly searching questions, to scare the boy into running as fast as he could in the opposite direction from the British Bulldogs. This was not someone who even fully understood the nasty agenda beneath their show of being simple patriots, let alone supported and wanted to promote it.

'I need names, Gregory. I accept that you yourself were not even in Lafferton, but you know who was, you have the names of people high up in this pathetic little organisation and who organised these hate crimes – because that is only one thing they'll be charged with. Hate crime, grievous bodily harm, intent to injure, causing an affray – we'll throw the book at them and they won't be bothering us for a good few years. So, if you're involved with them, you'd be sensible to get out fast. You don't want this sort of thing hanging round your neck when you try to get a career going, and it will. OK, so – tell me their names.'

He thought the boy was going to cry. His face was pale, he was rubbing his fingers together, his mouth working. It was the point at which Simon knew to take his foot off the pedal.

'Greg, you're OK ... you're not like this. And if you haven't got in deep, it won't matter. I know how these guys work – they're like cults, they brainwash you, they suck you in. It's happened to many more than you, don't worry. So – just give me some names, even a couple. Nothing's going to come back to you, they won't have the slightest idea how we got their details and police never ever reveal sources of information.' He leaned forward. 'That's a cast iron promise.'

Five minutes later, he was heading from the house, with three names, three e-mail addresses and one postal, having had a word with Philip Warren and told him to go easy on Greg.

'Let's go over this one step at a time. It's straightforward enough but we're deploying a large number of officers and we need to have their exact placement crystal clear.'

Mike Holmes had no laptop or screen, he had a whiteboard, a marker pen and a pointer. The room was packed with representatives of every group who had any connection with the following Saturday's Parade – uniform from both Lafferton and two adjacent forces, CID, the army, the Cathedral, the Prince of Wales's office and royal protection. The Acting Chief sat at the side, the Major in the front, arms folded.

Serrailler came in as the Super began and stayed at the back. He had received a note a few minutes before that two of the British Bulldog youths had been tracked down and brought in for questioning.

The timetable was gone over, minute by minute, there were no logistical problems, the police were clear about where they would be. The atmosphere in the room was businesslike and calm. Even Major Gardiner did not raise any queries other than minor clarifications.

Serrailler went forward.

'Mike, if I may ... I think we're all cautiously optimistic that things will run smoothly, as I remind you, they always have – we're proud of that. I can add another positive note – the group calling themselves the British Bulldogs, who were responsible for the violence and mayhem at the Gay Pride parade, are pretty small beer and based in Bevham. So far as we can discover, they only have one other sub-section, in the North of England, oddly enough. We now know the Bevham cell has around twenty five to thirty members, maximum and some of those are likely to be hangers on – the usual suspects who'd join a mother and toddler group if they thought it would bring some action. Two are on their way in now, one is likely to follow tonight and these are the ringleaders. So we're not going to let them cause any trouble next Saturday. But a more important point is that they wouldn't want to – this is a regiment of the British army on parade. These guys are scum but they are ultra-proud of being British and of all things British, especially the military. They are racist and homophobic, and they're on the look out for targets but the fusiliers are not among them.'

6

'Si, I'm about half an hour away and I hope there's a bottle open, we've had a foul journey down.'

'Bottle in the fridge. Who's we?'

'I'm bringing an old friend back – you won't remember Polly Attwater, we were at med school together. Her car's being towed back home in shame by the AA and she'll catch a train home tomorrow. So make it two bottles. How's Sam?'

'Are you driving as we speak?'

'Not really, I'm stationary in a long tailback.'

'Makes no difference, as well you know, so get off the bloody phone.'

Cat make a cross noise and disconnected.

Sam was in the doorway. 'What will happen to Greg?'

'Nothing.'

'You sure about that?'

'I am. But he had a wake-up call and I don't think he's going to be joining up with the Bulldogs. Don't worry, Sambo, I wouldn't shop him and anyway, he's done nothing criminal, just been stupid.'

'OK.' But he sounded doubtful. 'Better not tell Mum.'

'As if...'

'You on duty at the Colour Parade?'

'It's primarily uniform's responsibility but I'll be around.'

'Brett Forrester's Dad has a flat over the bank in the square. I'm going there.'

'Great viewpoint. Now – let's do a bit of a sprint round the house.'

Sam groaned and went to fetch the vacuum cleaner.

It was over an hour more before Cat and Polly arrived home.

'We hoovered,' Sam said. He gave his mother

a brief hug, and went upstairs, not in the mood to appear over-affectionate in company or be more than polite to unknown women.

Polly was almost as tall as Simon, with very short, very curly hair and a wide smile, which she gave him as he handed her a glass of Sauvignon.

'Conference worthwhile?'

'Yes,' Polly.

'Yes-ish.' Cat.

He laughed, sitting opposite and pushing back his flopping lock of hair. Polly was looking at him, then at Cat, then back again.

'I expected you to be more alike,' she said.

'Non-identical.'

'Sure, but where did the white-blonde hair come from?'

'Nobody knows.'

'A Scandinavian throw-back?'

'Out of a bottle?'

'Excuse me …' Simon threw the cork, which landed in Polly's glass.

'I feel,' Cat said, 'irresponsible. It was a bit

full-on. I heard more talks about aspects of death and dying in four days than in the whole of the rest of my career, and that drive was a nightmare ....' She raised her arms in the air. 'But I'm FREE! And I've come back to a clean and tidy house. Thanks, Bro. I know you are a tidiness freak but Sam is something else.'

Simon cooked steaks and opened a bottle but by nine, both women could hardly keep their eyes open. After she had shown Polly to the spare room, Cat came back down to look quickly through the post.

'Nice,' Simon said.

Cat gave him a sharp look.

'Married?'

'Divorced. You must know the name, surely.'

'No?'

'Giles Attwater?'

'Oh, good God, of course – great spin bowler, took four wickets off eleven balls in ...'

'Yeah, yeah. Anyway, that was him but the cricket field wasn't the only one he played.'

'Shame. Long time ago?'

'Si, I'm warning you …'

'What about?' He looked at her, widening his eyes. 'Maybe she'd like to stay over till Saturday, watch the Colour Parade?'

Cat went up to bed, shaking her head, though not exactly in disbelief. She knew her brother too well.

The phone woke him at ten past six the next morning.

'Can you get in here straight away, Gov?'

It had come as a disguised-voice message to the main switchboard, at six.

'You will regret tomorrow.'

'And that's it, Gov.'

'Shit,' Mike Philkpott said, walking in as it was being replayed.

'Major Gardiner just rang. They got exactly the same. Same time.'

'Is the Acting Chief available? We need to get round a table a.s.a.p.'

'He's got an interview Board at nine – can't be cancelled, there are four of them coming from out of the county, three of them have been staying overnight.'

'Right, we carry on and he can be contacted if it's necessary.' Serrailler thought for a second. 'I think we'd better not use any of the conference rooms, just in case. My office?'

'You, me, the Major, who will probably want to bring his sidekick. Ian Finch. That it? I'd like someone else backing me up ... DI Liscom I think. You want another CID.'

'Why?'

'Cover your back on this one, Simon, cover your back.'

Mike had experience in Northern Ireland. Serrailler trusted his judgment.

'Eight o'clock?'

Major Gardiner was coming from London and would not make it until nine at the earliest.

'Tell him we can liaise by phone while he's travelling?'

But Gardiner was insistent. He needed to be there.

'Alison, could you organise coffee for us please, and the usual crystal clear and wholesome tap water and decent biscuits?' Alison was always in by eight o'clock and logging into her computer.

'Will you need me?'

'No, probably not and you've got a lot on your plate.'

'You can say that again. Did your sister get back safely?'

'Yup. Brought an old friend home too. Rather nice.'

Alison rolled her eyes.

'When we start, will you make absolutely sure we're not interrupted – unless there's another warning message? Nothing else at all.'

The Major did not bring anyone with him but Serrailler's room was still overcrowded. He apologised.

'But we have to be secure and the conference rooms may not be. I hope this won't take long. Mike?'

'Firstly, we have no clue at all about this message. The voice was carefully disguised, the number wasn't traceable because this was a recording. There is nothing to indicate the reason for the warning. We're working in the dark unless we get another of them and even then …'

'Is this targeted at us or at the police, do you think?' Major Gardiner looked more worried but less distant than at the previous meeting. Simon thought the warning had come as a shock and that memories of all sorts of threats had kicked in – threats which had not been idle. The fusiliers had been in Afghanistan, and in the past had done several tours of Iraq. Security would always be an issue but it was easy to feel safer back on home ground.

'It could be either but far more likely to be the army I'm afraid. In the days of the IRA, bomb warnings were always sent to the police, no matter where they were planted or who was the target but those days are behind us, pretty much. The terrorist organisations in the mainland don't send warnings, they simply strike and the perpetrators are usually suicide bombers. I'm waiting to hear back from MI5 but this doesn't look like any sort of threat by Jihaddists.'

'Yet they would be the most likely people out to get us.'

'Yes.'

'What are everyone else's gut feelings? Simon?'

'That these are amateurs, though who or why I've no idea. The thing is, we could spend all day discussing who, or even why and get no further forward. That's unless other messages come in. What we need to talk about is our response, and yours.'

'We certainly can't cancel. That's out of the question.'

'Your call, Major,' Mike said, 'but I agree. That would be a last resort and I would always advise against. It sends out entirely the wrong signal.'

The Major drained his coffee, set the cup

down and drummed his fingers on the table for a second or two. They waited. Serrailler knew that he had not got to his present rank by being indecisive. He was not dithering, he was thinking.

'The details have all been public for a while. Date, route, timings.'

'This has never been a secret. The only info not given out to the public in detail has been the Prince of Wales's schedule. Do we know if St James's Palace have had this warning message?'

'They have not.'

'Would he be advised to cancel?'

'Absolutely not,' Major Gardiner said. 'And if he were he would probably take no notice.'

'Right,' Serrailler said, 'CID are working on the message, I've put a team onto making enquiries all over the shop but while we wait to see if they get anywhere. Meanwhile, unless something very significant happens, when we would take a view, we put as many more officers out there as we possibly can.'

'I'd like to double our Armed Response number,' Ian Finch said. 'We keep a low profile, as ever, but we will be on the spot, not waiting back here for a call.'

'And all for a pack of bloody jokers.'

'Indeed, but we can't take the chance of assuming that.'

'I wonder what you think about changing the timings, Major?' Mike Philpott asked.

'I think that would disappoint the people.'

'Not really ... they would simply wait a bit longer.'

'But,' Serrailler said, 'let's suppose for a moment that this is a bomb threat, and that the bomb is timed to explode as the Parade reaches the square, where the salute will be taken. At the moment that's scheduled for ten thirty. We make it eleven. The putative bomb would go off and do a hell of a lot of damage, probably kill people. That would spare the military but nothing else.'

'Listen, you're going to have sniffer dogs all over the shop in any case – they come with the royalty. We can close the square the night before – the afternoon before if you like. We will have officers on duty the whole time. The dogs can go in as early as possible and then again. No one will get near.'

'You're assuming this is a bomb. The word wasn't mentioned in the message.'

Mike Philipott leaned back. 'Nothing else causes that sort of carnage. Anything less, it will be dealt with before it starts. We prepare for the worst, whatever it takes.'

'This is such a damned waste of our time when there isn't likely to be a bomb or anything else. If these people only realised ...'

'They do,' Serrailler said. 'It's what they get off on, causing us the maximum amount of grief.'

Major Gardiner leaned forwards. 'Shall we take a view? I agree that this is almost certainly a hoax but I'm not prepared to chance it. Any more than you are. I am happy to put things back by thirty minutes, so long as the Prince's office agree, and the Cathedral are happy.'

'And that we are,' Simon said, not catching Mike Philpott's eye.

'Of course.'

'Good. It's our Parade, our call to ask if it's acceptable. I'll let you know the minute everyone has agreed, and just pray that they do.'

'Had you better phone from here, Major, time being short?'

'Can I have a secure room?'

'You can have this one.' Serrailler stood up.

'I'll hold it all until you give me the go ahead,' Mike Philpott said, 'and then organise everything here. Ian, are you happy?'

'I will be when it's sorted.'

'Just to repeat ... this is on a need to know basis only and at the moment, those who need to know are in this room. Even later, we keep the information from getting around the station and no one mentions it outside. Every possible source of leaks has to be stopped. Let my secretary know when you're done and she'll find one of us.'

Serrailler and the Super left Major Gardiner to make his calls in private. Twenty minutes later, he had confirmed that the new timing met with approval, under the circumstances.

'The Palace is happy because the Prince doesn't have any prior engagement, he's coming straight here and afterwards he's heading home to Gloucestershire, so the delay isn't a problem. Cathedral can do it – they will ask if the choir can fill in with some extra music and they won't tell the congregation until everyone is safely seated. There won't be any explanations – any mention of a threat to security and people start panicking. I've also spoken to the Lord Lieutenant's office – they're happy and there won't be any leaks from there. Thank you, gentlemen.'

The Major's car was waiting. As he emerged, the driver opened the door and saluted.

'Bit like royalty,' Mike Philpott said.

'Get to be Chief and this too could be yours.'

'Chief? In your dreams. I like a quiet life.'

Serrailler laughed, leaping two at a time up

the stairs. He had suddenly remembered Polly Attwater and whether she would like dinner that evening.

7

'Bad luck, I took her to the eight thirty train,' Cat said, laughing. 'And you wouldn't have got far, she has a bloke in tow – a Consultant she works with. I don't know any more, she was quite cagey.'

'Just thought she might need cheering up. Bit lonely here with only you and Sam.'

'Yeah, right. Glass of Prosecco?'

'No, I'll have a beer thanks. I had a message from the builders, by the way – the asbestos is all out of the flat but making good will take a couple of weeks longer than expected because of some problem with the roof timbers. Can you put up with me or shall I find a B and B?'

'Sure, there are some cheap ones down the Bevham Road. Idiot. Any excitements while

I've been away?'

He could not tell her about the Parade.

'Some unpleasant things in Grosvenor Place...'

'Those new houses behind security gates? I thought they paid a fortune for a private security firm.'

'Yes and it's failed them... Two houses were entered in the night, two women in adjacent houses have woken up to find a man in their bedroom. Their husbands were both away, which someone must have known.'

'I should look at the security firm if I were you.'

'No, really? You've been wasting your time as a doctor.'

'Seriously, Si – that's nasty – the sort of thing I get nightmares about...'

'Yes, I think you should upgrade your window locks here. The doors are fine. I'll get one of our guys to come over and advise – they're the experts.'

'There's no hurry so long as you're staying here but yes, please. I'll pay a lot for peace of mind.'

'Which the people of Grosvenor Place thought they were doing.'

Simon went into the den with his beer, and switched on the late news. He wished peace of mind was only a question of money.

He had offered to cook supper but Cat said she had been unwinding from the conference by doing a batch of food for the freezer, so they would have some of the chilli she made in huge quantities, because everyone asked for it so often.

The news of wars and disasters was almost over and the weather about to come up when Simon's phone rang.

'Our joker has rung again.' Mike Philpott said. 'Same voice. Slightly different message. *You're still going to regret it. Britain for the British.*

'Bloody bulldogs then. There must be a lot more of them than we suspected.'

'No, this is someone's double-bluff. Those guys wouldn't target the British army, as we've said.'

'So, what do they want?'

'To cause mayhem. What other reason could there be? Behind all genuine threats and warnings is always a demand for something but these jokers have made none and they would have to – we couldn't guess their agenda when we don't even know who they are.'

'There'll be another message, telling us what they want then.'

'No. they're hoaxers, Simon, they get a kick out of causing us grief and when better? This isn't like a threat to disrupt the Friday Farmer's Market. They know we have to take this seriously.'

'We'd have to take that seriously.'

'Yes, but it wouldn't be any big problem.'

'Have you phoned Gardiner?'

'He phoned me.'

'Then the AC will advise them to cancel.'

'No. I've spoken to him. They're both adamant. We go ahead as agreed. It's now become a matter of pride as well as everything else.'

'Mike, I don't want it to have us take our eyes off Grosvenor Place.'

'We haven't had any further incidents there.'

'We will. This sort of prowler doesn't stop, he bides his time and waits for his next opportunity and if we're not careful, we'll hand him one.'

'Listen, I need every man on the ground, from Friday night when we close the square. We have to have men on the whole route and up at the Cathedral, from dusk. It's a logistical bloody nightmare. I've got all leave cancelled, no one is off duty but there are only so many bodies to go round.'

'Such a big show of strength will be a deterrent in town. There won't be the usual Saturday night trouble. Capitalise on that. But Grosvenor Place is already keeping CID awake at night. If this man strikes again and there aren't enough uniform to provide a fast response he'll live to fight another day and this time he won't just stand there doing heavy breathing. He's clever, Mike. He will know only too well that his chances of getting away with it again are even better.'

'I don't care for them in general, but they could be helping us out here – so whatever happened to this private firm Grosvenor Place residents pay an arm and a leg for?'

'They backed out. They didn't look so good when major breaches of their so-called security happened.'

'Those guys,' Mike Philpott said, 'are all hat and no cattle.'

'So let's make sure we do better. I don't care if you're a couple of uniform short in the square, get them patrolling up there. If they keep a low profile, they might even catch him.'

8

Saturday morning. Sun. A light breeze, fluttering the flags. Lafferton en fete. The barriers which had blocked the square to allcomers were removed half an hour before the Colour Parade was scheduled to start, so far as most people knew, and the crowd filled it within minutes. The dais, on which the Prince of Wales would stand to take the salute, was covered by an awning, the whole area in front of it and taking in the route of the march-past, was cordoned off. Armed response vehicles were stationed inside and outside, snipers were in position on rooftops. But as ever, no one took any notice and the mood was buoyant. Excited children waved, hoisted up on shoulders.

Walkie-talkies squawked here and there. The royal car and its outriders, were ten minutes away.

Everything had been timed to the second, the soldiers lined up, band in front.

'Stand at – EASE!'

Clatter, stamp of a thousand boots.

They were only told now of the change. They would simply wait longer until the order came to move off. The sun was not hot. No one would faint.

Serrailler had come to the parade ground first. As the regiment moved off, he would go quickly out of the side gate and nip up one of the small lanes that led to the square, arriving before the parade. Plain clothes officers were mingling with the public, along the route, in the square, in the Cathedral. On a day like this, CID's role was to be eyes and ears.

He waited. The sun caught on medals, the band's instruments, cap badges. The parade ground was very still. A helicopter flew low overhead. From a single tree near to the main gates, a bird sang.

To everyone not in the know, which was most of them there, the wait seemed both endless and inexplicable, until, as the Cathedral clock struck the half hour, the Sergeant Major bawled the men to attention, the band struck up the regimental march, and the troops swivelled as one, and began to move off, out of the gates, into the road and up the hill, the crowds already pent up and now running to get alongside, shouting, waving, cheering them on.

From his vantage point in the Square Serrailler heard the first strains of the music and sent a message over to Mike Philpott. 'So far so ...'

The sun shone on the soldiers, up the hill, through the main streets and into the square, shone on the brass and silver, the cap badges and upturned faces, shone on the flag-waving children and the saluting Prince, on the flying gilded angels on the four corners of the Cathedral tower so that they caught fire, shone through the glorious stained glass windows into the Nave, full of patiently waiting military men and women, the families of the living soldiers and of the dead ones, and made azure and poppy red and violet lozenges on the stone flags.

The sound of the band floated in through the open East door at last and the Bishop and Dean and the robed choir moved off down the aisle towards it, and as the parade arrived and the band fell silent, the organ sounded the first notes of *Praise my Soul, the King of Heaven.*' The congregation rose to its feet with a rumble and a sigh like the sound of a wind rushing through poplars.

The square below was thronged with people talking and laughing and leaving, some for home, others to walk up towards the Cathedral to wait for the end of the Service and the sight of the regiment on its cheerful way back to the barracks.

And still, the sun shone.

Serrailler met up briefly with Mike Philpott as they headed out of the square. One of the Armed Response vehicles was stationed on the corner, men looking vigilant. They would not stand down until the military was safely back in the barracks.

Mike's phone buzzed and he answered, listened briefly, and rang off.

'The Prince's car has left and heading out of town.'

'Breathe easier then.'

'I tell you what – the number of excited kids around, I bet the army has a load of potential new recruits. Good PR, this sort of thing.'

'Maybe we should start.'

They parted, Serrailler to walk back to the station, Mike to the recreation ground behind the barracks, where the police vans that had brought in the extra men were parked. He would wait till everyone was back, debrief, congratulate, and then sign them off and away.

And still the sun shone.

Shone on the cap badges and medals and boot caps of the men marching back into the parade ground, and on the brass and silver instruments playing their last *'Hail and Farewell.'*

Shone on the Major, at the very back of the regiment.

Shone on the police car gliding into the parade ground behind the military and coming to a halt as the soldiers swivelled round and stood to attention. The car door opened and the man in police uniform climbed out, and began to walk quickly away, towards the open gates.

Perhaps someone should have shouted out to him that he had forgotten to close the police car door. Perhaps someone did. Perhaps no one did. Perhaps the man had already broken into a run and was out of sight, before there was a split second and then a roar and the crack of doom and a ball of fire exploding behind the soldiers who half-thought, the ones who had time to think anything at all, that this must be the end of the world.

Serrailler started to run instinctively, almost before the explosion was over, seeing the fireball and the smoke ahead as he went, shouting into his phone. He had been near the scene of a car bombing once before, as a rookie constable in the Met. The sound was unmistakeable, unforgettable.

In a side street close to the barracks, a motorbike waited, engine running, ready for off. Waited. Serrailler sprinted fast round the corner as a man came towards him, a man he would have swerved to avoid, if he had not been pulling off a police uniform jacket and dropping it as he went. Gut instinct told him. He blocked the man's way and threw himself on him, pinning his arms, knee in his stomach. Just ahead of them, the motor bike roared away, the noise melting into the mayhem and chaos in the barracks yard, blending with the scream of the oncoming sirens. Simon looked down. The man's face was contorted with pain. But Simon knew him. He had seen him before, and quite recently. He could not place him, or when, or where, but *he knew him*. He struggled to hold him down, kneeing hard as he spoke again, urgently, into his phone.

The air was thick with foul dark smoke now. There were bits like grit in Simon's mouth. He heard screams. Shouts. And the sirens, blaring nearer, rounding the corner, ambulances, fire engines, police cars, streaming in one after another. He had asked for urgent assistance and got it, two uniform leaping out of their car as it slewed to a halt, relieving Serrailler to stand up, while they handcuffed the man and dragged him to his feet. He was breathless, chalk white, but his eyes, as he looked briefly into Simon's, were full of a terrible pride and triumph.

I know you, Simon thought, looking back. I know you.

'Name?' one of the uniform was asking. They had the man against the railings now.

For a second, he did not answer. Serrailler noticed that his hands were shaking, even restrained by the cuffs.

'You heard. I need your name. Now.'

A mutter.

'Speak up.'

'Anthony Barber.'

A flash-bulb in Serrailler's brain, shocking him so that for a second, he could not have spoken or moved.

'Jesus Christ.' Though the words were only in his head.

Behind them, the noise and the smoke and the smell and the pandemonium grew louder and the sirens came on, and on, screeching round the corner and through the gates, into the carnage. Overhead, the air ambulance helicopter chatttered down.

9

Serrailler watched the arrest car move off before walking into the parade ground, and immediately turning away. He was neither doctor, paramedic nor fire officer, he had no responsibility for the military, and the chaos was bad enough, without one spare Detective Chief Superintendent adding more. But as he turned, he caught sight of Mike Philpott, in shirt sleeves, a few yards from the back of the bomb-carrying stolen squad car, talking into his phone. He caught sight of Simon and beckoned.

His face was grey, with smoke and dust and shock. Simon touched his shoulder.

'Twenty two men dead, thirty four injured, fourteen very seriously, the others fairly seriously. More walking wounded with minor injuries.'

An ambulance siren and its blue light started up close to them, and went racing out, followed by another. A second air ambulance was coming in.

'Press,' Serrailler said. 'They'll want statements from Gardiner, and from us.'

'I'm getting men down now to man the gates. We don't want press vans and cameras in here yet. Jesus wept.' They both looked at a stretcher carrying a sheeted figure, blood already seeping through the fabric.

'Whoever did this ....'

'I know who did it,' Serrailler said. 'Just not why. You'd better come back to the station with me now. They're coping here.'

Mike nodded. It was only when Simon glanced sideways at him as he started the engine that he realised the Super was without his jacket and that he had blood down the front and sleeves of his shirt.

'No, it isn't me.' Philpott said, 'I was one

of the first in there. The guy had been blown up in the air by the blast. He was lying in my path. I bent down on a reflex before I saw there wasn't much left of him.'

It was gone seven o'clock before Simon could get downstairs. The aftermath of the bombing had taken up the time of everyone in the station, they were stretched to the limit, a Press Conference with full media attendance had taken place, to go out on the early evening News on all channels, the car park outside was crowded with press vans and cars. Lafferton, in a state of shock and disruption, needed calm policing and reassurance. But Serrailler did not forget. He carried it in his mind. He waited, waited, pent-up, until he could get ten free minutes.

Then he went downstairs.

Alison Barber was sitting on the bench in the holding cell, staring at the floor, her face in shadow. She wore a pale pink shirt, with a navy jumper round the shoulders, sleeves tied together. Jeans. Bright converse trainers.

An ordinary woman in her late thirties. A woman people saw every day on the streets of Lafferton. A woman you might not remember a second time.

A woman Serrailler had seen, and to whom he had spoken, every working day for the last eighteen months.

A woman he had liked. Respected. Praised for her efficiency and dedication, her organisational skills, her meticulous attention to detail. Her pleasantness. Her even-temper. Her kindness to everyone who came into her office.

Her kindness to him.

He nodded to the duty officer beside him to unlock the door. He could have asked her to go into an interview room, except that it was not his case, he had to keep away. He was not interviewing Alison Barber, he just wanted to confront her. Look her straight in the face. Ask her. Just ask. And tell her. Others would do the rest.

She started up as he came in then took a step away from the bench.

Serrailler remained by the door. He did not want to get any closer to her. He was cold and calm but still he did not trust himself.

He said. 'Listen to me. This afternoon twenty two soldiers were blown up and killed, not all of them instantaneously. Several dozen more were seriously injured. Two of those have since died in hospital. Others almost certainly will. Every single person on the parade ground is suffering from extreme shock and distress. Every one of them will suffer from post-traumatic stress, possibly for the rest of their lives, even with expert help. Men's lives have been lost or ruined. Men's families have been torn apart. Men's futures have been destroyed. The regiment, and the emergency forces, and the police, will never get over this. They will live with the nightmare of what happened until the end of their days. Lafferton will never forget it. The entire place is reeling. People are huddled on the streets crying. People are wandering about, stopping and talking to whoever will listen to them. Nothing will ever quite 'get back to normal' ever again.

And you did this, Alison Barber. You and your husband, and someone else we have not yet picked up but will. You or your husband will give us his name and we will bring him in.

You did this. I have nothing whatsoever to say to you because if I opened my mouth to begin, I would never stop and I would appall myself that I could use such terms. I am not going to dignify you with the attention. You'll get plenty. But I have one question. Not how – we've found the bug in my office, we know you listened in to everything about the planning of the parade, and passed it straight on. We will know about the car and the bomb and the hows and the whats. That's the straightforward part. Just the why. I think you owe it to me – though God alone knows, you owe it to far more people than me, because I haven't suffered in all this. Still, I employed you when you came for the job, in order to infiltrate the police and pursue your agenda. I worked with you. I liked you. Above all, I trusted you. This is all about trust, without which none of us would be able to function, and which you comprehensively betrayed.

So – why?'

He could not read anything into her expression. There was a blank, a deadness, in her eyes, the way she looked at him, without blinking or glancing away.

'Listen. You'll say what you like, or not, when you go in there, but that won't be me, I want and can have nothing to do with this. But while you're on your own with me here, God in heaven, you owe it. *Tell me why.*'

There was a long silence. He could hear someone shouting outside in the lobby. Silence again. He was clenching his fists so tightly the muscle of his upper arm began to ache.

'I had two brothers, two men I loved very dearly and who were my only family along with my sister, since my parents died in an accident, together. I had one brother-in-law. My sister's husband. They were all in the fusiliers. Three of them. And they are all dead. They were all murdered in Afghanistan. You'd say they died for their country. I'd say they were sacrificed by the British Army in a useless cause.'

'You don't know what I would say. I'm sorry for those deaths, but is that an excuse for blowing several dozen other soldiers to bits? An eye for an eye? Tell me how exactly that has helped your dead men?'

Her face did not change but he saw something in her eyes, a glint of passionate feeling, of hatred, of rage.

'It helps me,' she said.

He had to get out. If he had not he would have killed her. The officer outside locked up and Serrailler bolted, seeing nothing, seeing no one, along the corridor and up the stairs and out through the swing doors into the open air, across the front car park, crammed with its vehicles, and round the corner into the street, where he stopped and leaned against the railings, his heart pounding, feeling as if he was about to vomit. He did not. He took deep breaths and they steadied him. But it was a long time before he felt completely in control of himself, and safe enough to drive home.

Cat was sitting in a deckchair, the radio on the grass beside her. She switched it off as he walked over to her.

He threw his jacket down, and then himself and lay with his eyes closed, feeling the late afternoon sun on his face, seeing a parade ground full of the dead and the dying, hearing the sounds, the sirens, the cries and the shouting, smelling the smoke and the blind terror and panic. Tasting them.

Cat brought him large whisky and he sat and swigged it in one.

'Three more of the injured are dead,' she said.

Nothing more.

'Where's Sam?'

'His room. He's OK, we talked. Maybe you could see him a bit later.'

Simon nodded.

He felt the whisky run through his veins. After a moment, it hit some spot in him, his gut or his brain, and blazed up, and he bent forward, head on his arms, and began to sob.